PETER POWERS ™

and His Not-So-Super Powers!

D0369517

PETER POWERS™
and His Not-So-Super Powers!

By Kent Clark
& Brandon T. Snider
Art by Dave Bardin

Little, Brown and Company
New York Boston

Copyright © 2016 by Hachette Book Group, Inc.
PETER POWERS is a trademark of Hachette Book Group.
Cover and interior art by Dave Bardin
Cover design by Christina Quintero
Cover copyright © 2016 by Hachette Book Group, Inc.

Little, Brown and Company
Hachette Book Group
1290 Avenue of the Americas, New York, NY 10104
Visit us at lb-kids.com

Originally published in hardcover and ebook by Little, Brown and Company in October 2016
First Trade Paperback Edition: March 2017

Little, Brown and Company is a division of Hachette Book Group, Inc. The Little, Brown name and logo are trademarks of Hachette Book Group, Inc.

The publisher is not responsible for websites (or their content) that are not owned by the publisher.

The Library of Congress has cataloged the hardcover edition as follows:
Names: Clark, Kent. | Snider, Brandon T., author. | Bardin, Dave (Illustrator), illustrator.
Title: Peter Powers and his not-so-super powers! / by Kent Clark & Brandon T. Snider ; art by Dave Bardin.
Description: First edition. | Boston ; New York : Little, Brown and Company, 2016. | Series: Peter Powers ; [1] | Summary: "When Captain Tornado begins robbing banks, will Peter Powers and his totally lame superpowers step up to save the day?" —Provided by publisher.
Identifiers: LCCN 2016010295 | ISBN 9780316359320 (hardback) | ISBN 9780316359368 (ebook) | ISBN 9780316359337 (library edition ebook)
Subjects: | CYAC: Superheroes—Fiction. | Ability—Fiction. | Family life—Fiction. | Humorous stories. | BISAC: JUVENILE FICTION / Action & Adventure / General. | JUVENILE FICTION / Humorous Stories. | JUVENILE FICTION / Readers / Chapter Books.
Classification: LCC PZ7.1.C594 Pc 2016 | DDC [Fic]—dc23
LC record available at https://lccn.loc.gov/2016010295

ISBNs: 978-0-316-35934-4 (pbk.), 978-0-316-35936-8 (ebook)

Printed in the United States of America

LSC-C

10 9 8 7 6 5 4 3 2 1

Contents

CHAPTER ONE
My "Super" Family

My name is Peter Powers. And I have superpowers.

I know what you're thinking: *How cool!* Or maybe: *I want superpowers!* But trust me, you really don't. Especially if you have a super *lame* power like mine.

I guess you want to know what my superpower is, don't you? Well, my superpower is—*ugh*, this is *reeeally* embarrassing—I can make ice cubes with my fingertips.

See! You're laughing. No one respects my powers—or *me*! Everybody laughs. But you know who laughs at me the most? My family.

Well, okay, not my mom and dad. They're actually pretty nice and supportive, but I know what they're really thinking. They probably *have* to be nice to me because of some secret parent code. Like me, my parents have superpowers. Unlike me, they're *actual* superheroes. They have capes and masks and everything.

2

They protect Boulder City, which is where we live.

If you haven't heard of my mom, well, she can fly. She's faster than a jet. I've even heard rumors that she can fly around the whole world in less than an hour. (I should ask her if that's true.) So awesome.

Then there's my dad. He can control fire with his mind! How cool is that? Or I guess that would be the opposite of cool, but in a totally rad way. His fire powers make it so he can fly and shoot blasts of flame. I wish that was my power.

So I guess the only people who actually make fun of me are my brother and sister. But they do it a *lot*.

My older brother, Gavin, is the worst. He's fifteen years old and always playing pranks on me. Gavin has a superpower too: He can make copies of himself. So instead of having just *one* bully for an older brother, sometimes I have *five*. Yesterday, he went into my room and multiplied, and the five Gavins stapled all my underwear to the ceiling. (When there's five of him, it's easy for them to climb on one another's shoulders to do stuff.)

Then there's my younger sister, Felicia. She is super strong. One time, our car got a flat tire, and she picked up the whole van so Dad could fix it. She didn't even break a sweat! I bet if she used both hands, she could pick up our house.

On top of being strong, she's also really smart. She makes straight As. You'd think she'd be nicer, since she has everything. But she makes fun of me too. Like, if there's one last cookie, she'll be like, "You wanna arm wrestle for it?" Yeah, right.

Oh, and did I mention that she's only nine? So yeah, I get bullied by my nine-year-old sister. *Not cool.*

Even my baby brother, Ben, has a

superpower more awesome than mine. And he's only two years old! He can turn *invisible*. He doesn't make fun of me, but that's probably because he can barely speak. Once he starts talking, he'll probably be just as bad.

At least I have my grandpa Dale. He's a retired superhero. He doesn't get around much on account of being in a wheelchair, but he and I watch a lot of movies together. He's pretty much my best friend in our house.

You probably think having a whole family with superpowers is neat or cool or super amazing. But it's not.

Not when I have the crummiest power in

the house. Not when my brother and sister pick on me constantly. And definitely not when I tried to fight a *supervillain* to get some respect.

What's that? You haven't heard that story? I better start at the beginning. It all began over breakfast....

CHAPTER TWO
Bad Breakfast

"Hey, *squirt*," Gavin said, messing up my hair. My parents always make us eat breakfast together since they aren't always home for dinner. You know, because they "work" nights as superheroes.

"Don't call me *squirt*," I growled. I was having a bad morning. Probably because Gavin had hidden all my clean underwear again. He loves pranks.

"Boys, play nice," Dad said. Dad tossed

several pieces of bread into the air and toasted them with fire from his hand. He set the toast down on the table. "What else could I cook for breakfast? *Hmmm…* Anyone want waffles?"

"Honey, please don't make a mess," Mom said, floating into the kitchen. "Last time you made waffles, I spent all day cleaning batter off the ceiling." My mom used to be a pilot for the air force, but she could fly faster than any of their jets on her own. Why couldn't *that* have been my power?

I was reaching for a piece of toast when I was lifted into the air. With one hand, Felicia held my chair (with me in it!) over

her head while she took a piece of toast.
"Out of my way, squirt," Felicia said.

"Don't call me *squirt*," I growled.

"Put your brother down, young lady,"
Mom said.

"Fine," Felicia said. When Mom wasn't
looking, Felicia stuck her tongue out at me.

I put a piece of toast on my plate and
reached for the butter and jelly. That's
when Gavin copied himself. Gavin #1 took

the butter, and Gavin #2 took the jelly.
Both of them smiled and said, "Thanks,
squirt."

"*Sqit!*" my baby brother, Ben, tried to
say. He swung his spoon, sending apple-
sauce flying into my face. "*Sqit!*"

"*Don't call me squirt!*" I shouted at
everyone.

"Peter Patrick Powers!" Dad said. "There
is *no* shouting at the breakfast table."

"But—" I started.

"No buts, young man," my mom added.
"Apologize to everyone this instant."

"Sorry," I mumbled. I crossed my arms
and tried to swallow my anger.

Felicia and Gavin gave each other a

low five under the table. My grandpa Dale wheeled into the kitchen. He scowled at my brother and sister. "You two are up to no good as usual, I see. Mischief is the road to evil. Keep acting the way you do, and you'll end up being the bad guys!"

"Come on, Dale," my father said to his father-in-law.

"They will!" Grandpa said. I silently agreed.

My brother and sister shrugged and left the room. But not before Gavin #2 grabbed the toast off my plate and ran after the others.

"You know," Grandpa said to me, "if you want your brother and sister to be nicer to you, you need to earn their respect."

"How do I do that?" I asked.

"That's easy." He smiled. "Defeat a supervillain."

CHAPTER THREE
Lunch Plans

"I have to defeat a supervillain!" I said at lunch the next day.

Chloe and Sandro looked at me with funny faces. They're my best friends and the only people in our school who know my secret. My family likes to keep our powers hush-hush. It's what we call a "secret identity."

Chloe put down her PB&J sandwich. She's the smart one in our group. "What are you talking about, Peter?"

"I want my brother and sister to stop being mean to me, and the only way to do that is to get them to respect me. And the only way to get their respect is to defeat a supervillain."

"Are you going to use your"—Sandro wiggled his finger and whispered—

"superpower?" He's the clown of the group, but he always supports my decisions—even the bad ones.

"*Shhhh!*" I whispered, looking around to make sure no one else in the school cafeteria had heard him. "That's supposed to be top secret."

"Then you shouldn't have told Sandro." Chloe smiled. "He's not very good at keeping secrets."

"It's true, I'm not," Sandro agreed.

"But seriously, how are you going to take down a supervillain?" Chloe asked.

I shrugged. "I don't know. I haven't figured out that part yet."

"Sounds like a lot of work," Sandro said. "Who cares how your brother and sister treat you?"

"I do! You don't know what it's like to live with them!" I said. "They torment me day and night. If they respected me, they'd leave me alone."

"I doubt that," Chloe said. "No matter what I do, my older sister always steals my stuff. That's what siblings do."

"I guess I need a plan," I said. "First, I need to *find* a supervillain. Where do you find bad guys?"

"My mom says the electric company is evil," Chloe said. "But I think that's because our bill is always so high."

"Hey, I know," Sandro said. "I was watching the news last night. A super-villain named Captain Tornado has been robbing banks all over town. He's already robbed three—that means there's only two left. We should go to one of them after school and hang out. If he shows up, you zap him. Then—*bam!*—you're an instant hero."

"That is a terrible idea," Chloe said.

"You mean a *great* idea!" I said. I began to daydream of stopping a bank robbery, defeating Captain Tornado, and earning the respect of the entire town.

What could possibly go wrong?

CHAPTER FOUR
Super Showdown

There he was, Boulder City's most famous supervillain: *Captain Tornado!*

I couldn't believe it. I was finally face-to-face with a real-life bad guy! I had arrived at the bank just in time to catch him in the act. Not only that, but my powers had become mysteriously supercharged. I felt invincible. It was time to show that windy weirdo that I wasn't messing around.

"Back off, *blowhard!*" I said, shooting an ice bolt at Captain Tornado.

"Who are you?" asked Captain Tornado. "Freezey the Snowboy? HA-HA-HA!"

"The name is Peter Powers!" I said proudly. "Remember it. I'm the person who's putting you on ice."

"Oh, I'll try," said Captain Tornado. "If you can stop me, Snowboy!"

Captain Tornado launched several mini-tornadoes. They were headed right toward me! Thankfully, I was prepared. I moved to the right, then leaped to the left. I avoided each tiny twister with ease. All those years of playing dodgeball in gym class had finally paid off.

But the battle wasn't over yet. I could

feel my superpowers getting stronger and stronger. It was time for my big moment.

"This should take the *wind* out of your sails!" I said. I let loose with everything I had. My powers trapped Captain Tornado in a big block of ice. I did it! I defeated my very first bad guy! And it wasn't even that hard!

"This won't hold me forever," Captain

Tornado sneered. "By the way, your puns are *terrible*!"

"I'll have to work on my jokes now that I am the world's greatest superhero!" I said with confidence.

"But jokes or no jokes, protecting the city always comes first!"

"You think you're so great and powerful, don't you?" Captain Tornado said. "If you're so smart, why don't you tell me what the capital of Nebraska is?"

"Huh?" Why was Captain Tornado asking me that? Was this a trick? Everyone in the bank was staring, waiting for my answer. I couldn't let them down.

But I had no idea what the capital was. Nebraska City? If I wasn't the smartest hero, I was still the most powerful! I mustered every bit of energy I had. I raised my hands and shouted, "Ice blast!"

But nothing happened. Nothing except

the usual—little ice cubes came out of my fingertips and dropped sadly to the floor.

"You're not a hero. Heroes have *real* superpowers. You're just a little baby who makes ice cubes," said Captain Tornado. "*Ice Cube Baby!* Now tell me, what is the capital of Nebraska!"

"Huh?" I said. What was going on?

"Wake up," Captain Tornado hissed. "I said *wake up*, young man!"

"Wake up, Peter Powers!" repeated my teacher, Miss Dullworth. She was staring right at me.

"*GAH!*" I shouted, jumping up from my desk like a spider had bitten my butt. I wasn't at the bank. I never had been. I was in school with drool on my face. I had fallen asleep in class and dreamed the whole thing. Now everyone was laughing at me. The only thing *super* about this was how *super* embarrassed I was.

CHAPTER FIVE
Bank Business

After school, Chloe, Sandro, and I walked to the closest unrobbed bank. If Captain Tornado tried to rob it, I wanted to be ready and waiting for him. At least that was the plan. As we got closer, I started to think this wasn't such a good idea.

"This is a really bad idea," said Chloe, as if reading my mind. "You are so *not* ready to fight a real supervillain, Peter."

I wanted to disagree, but my friend wasn't wrong. This could go very badly if I wasn't careful.

"I totally disagree," Sandro said to Chloe. "Remember the time Peter stuck a cat in a tree just so he could save it? That was a great idea!"

"No, it wasn't," I said. "Operation: Kitty Time resulted in me having my face scratched almost completely off!"

"Peter, at least tell me you have an *actual* plan," Chloe said.

"Of course I do!" I lied. "But my plan is very detailed and complicated, so I can't tell you everything about it."

Chloe gave me the side eye. She wasn't buying it. She knew me too well.

As we walked into the bank, the snooty bank manager gave us a glare. Mr. Kramer continued to watch us like a hawk as we pretended to be waiting for a parent. The manager looked like an angry toothpick with a mustache, and as he stared, I became even more nervous. But people (and their hard-earned money) were depending on me! I had to be brave. Right?

Mr. Kramer straightened his tie and started walking our way. Uh-oh.

"Here comes the manager! What do we do now, smarty-pants?" asked Chloe.

"Be cool," I whispered.

"That's easy for you to say, Mr. I-Can-Make-Ice-Cubes!" Sandro whispered.

"May I help you with something?" asked Mr. Kramer. He was smiling, but his eyes couldn't hide his annoyance.

"We were...uh..." I was terrible at coming up with stories on the spot. "Uh...,"

"This is a *bank*"—the manager squinted—"*not* a playground."

"It's not? Oh. That makes more sense. We were wondering where the swings and slides were," Chloe said. "Our mistake. We're going now." Chloe tried to leave, but I caught her hand and gave her a pleading look.

31

"I think I need to contact your parents," scoffed Mr. Kramer. This guy wasn't fooling around. My parents would be furious if they knew what I was up to. But saving the city came first—especially when it meant earning some respect.

But then Sandro opened his big mouth. "Captain Tornado is on the loose! You do realize that, right? He could be heading here right now!" he shouted. So much for being cool. It was time to come clean.

"We aren't sure, but you might be in terrible danger, Mr. Kramer," I said. "A supervillain named Captain Tornado has been robbing every bank in town. We think your bank is next on his list."

"You silly little boy. You have been reading too many of those *comical* books with the colorful art!" Mr. Kramer laughed. "Thank you for your concern, but we have top-notch security."

"I think you mean *comic* books," I said respectfully. "And your security doesn't *look* top-notch." I pointed to the security guards in the corners. They'd fallen asleep and were snoring like freight trains.

WHOOSH!

Suddenly, a giant gust of wind blew the front doors of the bank wide open. Papers went swirling everywhere, and Mr. Kramer's hair flew right off his head!

A roar filled the room as Captain Tornado arrived. His blustery presence even woke up the sleeping security guards.

"You know how this goes," Captain Tornado announced. "Don't try anything. Just give me all the money, and I won't use my powers to blow this bank all the way to Oz!"

I ducked behind Chloe and Sandro. Then I put on my homemade hero mask and pulled up my hood. I didn't have a real costume, but I still had to keep my secret identity secret.

"NOT SO FAST, CAPTAIN TORNADO!" is what I *wanted* to say. But it didn't quite come out of my mouth that way. Instead, I said, *"FAST NOT SO, TORNADO CAPTAIN!"*

It was far from my finest

moment. I was so scared, my knees were clicking together like two broomsticks. But it was time for me to stand my ground and be the hero I was meant to be—that is, if I didn't poop my pants first.

CHAPTER SIX
The Real Showdown

"Who are *you*?" asked Captain Tornado. He stared at me with a rather confused look on his face. Then he looked around the bank. "Am I on one of those joke-situation reality shows?"

"I'm a...a...superhero?" I gulped. My statement came out like a question.

"Seriously?" Captain Tornado asked. "You can't be older than ten or eleven. I can't fight you. That's child abuse."

"Well, uh...I'm older and...uh, tougher

than I look," I said, almost in a whis-
per. This was *not* going as well as I had
hoped.

"His name is POWER BOY!" Sandro
shouted. "Want to find out why? You may
not like the answer." Sandro's witty banter
was definitely better than mine. "It's
because he has *powers*." Or maybe not.

"I've got this," I said to Sandro.

But Sandro has a big mouth. Once he
starts talking, he can't seem to stop. "But
they're not very useful. He just makes ice
cubes with his fingers," he added.

"What. Are. You. Doing?" I asked
Sandro through gritted teeth.

"He's going to find out sooner or later,"

whispered Sandro. "This way he's not expecting much, and you can really impress him with your skills!"

It wasn't a bad idea. The problem was that I didn't have any skills. Suddenly, it occurred to me that I should have practiced *before* I decided to take on my first bad guy.

"Listen, kid," Captain Tornado said gently. "You're out of your element. This won't end well for you. So please head outside and let me go about my business." Then he walked past me and made his way toward the bank vault.

The security guards tried to tackle Captain Tornado. With a swish of the supervillain's fingers, two tornadoes picked up the security guards and tossed them into garbage cans.

Captain Tornado strolled over to the bank vault. Then he used his powers to suck the door open. He stopped to smile at all the money. He was about to take everything!

I had to act fast. I closed my eyes and concentrated, squeezing my fist as tightly

as I could. I could feel it getting colder and colder.

"I can do this," I said to myself. "I CAN DO THIS!"

Opening my hand, I aimed it at Captain Tornado. A single ice cube shot right out of my fingers and hit him in the forehead.

"Whoa!" said Chloe. "You did it!" Sandro and Chloe gave each other a high five. They believed in me—but did I believe in myself?

Captain Tornado just rubbed his forehead and said, "Hey, that almost hurt. Good for you, kid. One day, you might be really good at this hero stuff. But not today."

I couldn't believe the supervillain was giving me a pep talk.

"Okay, I've got work to do," he said. He

flicked a mini-tornado in my direction, and it pushed me back toward the wall. "Go home, kid. Do your homework. Eat your veggies. And make something of yourself. Crime doesn't pay…well, unless you rob banks."

With a wave of his hands, Captain

Tornado made a massive whirlwind. It began to suck each and every bill out of the bank vault, fly it across the bank, and then stack it neatly in his getaway car. His powers were awesome!

"Peter, do something!" pleaded Chloe. "The money I made doing chores was

in that vault. I was saving it up to buy a video game!"

Making that one ice cube took everything I had. I was so tired, I could have fallen asleep right there. But I needed to do something. Not just for the city, but for my friends. I stepped between Captain Tornado and the door.

"I-I can't let you leave," I said. "Not until you return the money."

"Come on, kid," Captain Tornado said. "Enough is enough. You lost. Now please move."

This wasn't how I'd pictured the showdown in my head. Captain Tornado stood there for a moment, staring me down. I had no idea what he was thinking. Was it possible I had pushed him too far? Was he going to hurt us? I'd forgotten that super-heroics always end with a big fight. I'd never been in a fight before.

Suddenly, a familiar voice shouted behind me.

"This ends here and now, Tornado!" the voice cried out. Now I was in *big* trouble. I didn't know who to be more scared of: the supervillain... or my *mom*.

CHAPTER SEVEN
Trouble

My mom was standing there in her full hero stance, ready to do battle with Captain Tornado—until she saw me.

Then a car-sized tornado slammed into her, punching her into the wall. "What are *you* doing here?!" Mom asked. I could tell she hadn't expected to see me by the shocked look on her face, *plus* she was yelling. I immediately knew I was in big trouble.

"You *know* this little hero-in-the-making?" Tornado asked. Mom didn't answer because it would blow her secret identity. The silence was almost worse. When a mom is silent, it's *never* a good thing.

But Mom's a total professional when it

comes to being a hero. So handling Captain Tornado was her first order of business. I may have distracted her, but she recovered fast. She flew at Captain Tornado and grabbed him. "Sorry to put a crimp in your day, but I need to take you to jail."

"Maybe next time," he said. Captain Tornado waved his arms, creating an army of twisters headed straight for me, Chloe, and Sandro. My mom leaped into action. She flew across the room and deflected the twisters with ease, sending them back toward Captain Tornado and knocking him down.

"Are you okay?" Mom asked. Chloe and Sandro nodded.

"Yes," I said. I could see it in her eyes: She was disappointed in me. That was almost worse than her being angry.

"I want all of you to stay put. This is a

very *dangerous* situation. It's important that you listen to me," Mom said. "Do you understand?"

"He's escaping!" yelled Sandro, pointing to Captain Tornado. He was making his getaway. This was all my fault. I had to stop him. I had to fix this. I had an idea.

"Captain Tornado put all the money in his car. If we let him go, he'll drive away and we can track his license plate," I shouted.

"The car's not for driving, kid. It's for storage," Captain Tornado said. He'd heard me. On the long list of hero stuff I needed to learn, being quiet was another.

Captain Tornado used his powers to

conjure up a giant vortex of wind. The cyclone swept him and his car full of stolen money high into the sky. I could tell my mom was hesitating between going after the bad guy and staying to make sure I was okay. Of course, she stayed.

In no time at all, Captain Tornado and his car of stolen money disappeared into the clouds.

"I'm really sorry—" I began.

"Don't say another word," Mom said. I could tell she wasn't happy. When Dad arrived on the scene, I was doubly embarrassed.

"Hey there! Sorry for the delay. I was held up on the other side of town with a

bunch of mind-controlled gorillas and—
Peter?!" Dad sputtered. "What's going on
here?"

"Honey, would you mind escorting
Chloe and Sandro home? Peter and I need
to have a little talk."

Chloe and Sandro had that "hope
you're not grounded for life" look on
their faces as my dad escorted them out.
I stayed with Mom as she spoke to the
bank manager (who was still looking for
his toupee) and made sure everyone was
safe. Soon the police showed up to handle
the situation, and we finally headed
home.

"Mom, let me explain," I started. But as

soon as I opened my mouth, I stumbled. I didn't know what to say.

I thought I could handle the superhero lifestyle. I wanted to show my family that I wasn't just a little baby ice maker, but I was so embarrassed that it left me totally speechless.

"I know you want to be a hero, Peter, and I know you want to help. I'm very proud of you for taking the initiative, but you're simply not ready. Your powers haven't developed. You need proper training. And you are far too young." My mom took a deep breath. "Today, you entered a very dangerous situation that could have turned out very badly for everyone. And worse, you brought your friends too. They could have been seriously hurt. You've left me with no choice."

Oh no, I thought. *No no no no no!* She wouldn't, she couldn't! She's going to, isn't she? She's going to DOOM me and ruin my entire life. Just when I thought the day couldn't get any worse.

"You're grounded," Mom said firmly.

"No TV, no Internet, no phone, no video games. For a month."

My life was *officially* over.

CHAPTER EIGHT
A Quiet Dinner

No one spoke during dinner. Not a single word. It was super awkward. I think everyone was afraid to talk about what happened at the bank. I know I was. But once dessert was finished, Felicia couldn't help herself.

"Peter, why did you think you could face off against Captain Tornado alone? That's so crazy! You don't even have the right powers to hurt him!" Felicia said. Then Gavin got in on the action, of course.

"I would have made a bunch of copies of myself," he explained, acting out his faulty plan. "And then I would have jumped all over him until he was like, *'NOOOO! Gavin, you're overpowering me! You're the best superhero in the universe!'* And then I would have—"

"You weren't there!" I shouted, cutting Gavin off. My family seemed shocked at my outburst. I didn't mean to yell, but I couldn't stand listening to my brother any longer.

"Felicia and Gavin, it's time for homework," Mom said, escorting my grumpy siblings out of the room.

Dad and I sat for a moment, staring at

each other. We hadn't talked since the incident. I didn't know if he was going to strangle me or just tell me how disappointed he was. His silence made me nervous.

"Keep your chin up, Peter," Dad said, comforting me. "You've got heart. And you'll get there—*eventually*. But for now, please remember, you're just too young."

Dad cleared the dishes from the table and patted me on the back. I could tell I'd let him down. After he left the room, I sat there in silence for a while, thinking about everything.

"COMIN' THROUGH!" Grandpa said, bursting into the dining room in his wheelchair.

"You missed dinner, Grandpa," I told him.

"No, I didn't. I ate dinner at three o'clock! Then I took a nap." Grandpa rolled his wheelchair beside me. "Ahhh. My grandpa senses are tingling again. Is everything okay?"

"Not quite, Grandpa," I said. "I tried to defeat a supervillain, but it didn't go as planned."

"Why would you do something like that?!"

"Because you told me to!" I said.

"I did?" asked Grandpa.

"You did," I said, "but I failed."

"Well, why did you go and listen to me? I'm just a silly old man in a wheelchair," Grandpa said, giggling. "Don't worry, Peter, you'll get 'em next time! There's a lesson in everything. But it's up to you to find it. And remember—no matter what happens, tomorrow is a new day!"

Grandpa grabbed the cookie jar off

the counter and wheeled himself out of the room.

I cleaned up the rest of the dining room and went to bed, thinking about what Grandpa had said: *Tomorrow is a new day*. Hopefully, I'd do tomorrow better than I did today.

CHAPTER NINE
Friends?

It was lunchtime. And even though they were serving tacos (my favorite), I didn't have much of an appetite. I was wracked with guilt about what had happened at the bank.

I grabbed my tray and found a seat. I was so stuck in my head, I didn't notice I had company. Not until Chloe plunked her tray down right next to me and said, "Hello? Earth to Peter Powers! You here?"

"Hey," I said, picking at my taco.

Chloe started devouring her mac and cheese. We sat there eating our lunches in silence for almost a whole minute. Then Chloe piped up. "So, are you not going to talk to me or what?"

"I didn't think *you'd* want to talk to *me* after everything that happened yesterday," I said, bracing myself for her response. I knew what was coming. She was going to tell me I was a failure as a friend and as a superhero.

Make it quick, I thought.

"What are you talking about?" asked Chloe.

"Aren't you embarrassed to be my friend?" I asked back.

"Not at all," said Chloe.

"Peter!" said Sandro, putting his tray down across from me. My friend placed a delicious-looking chocolate dessert in front of me. "I got you the last cupcake! Oh man, it looks so good I almost ate it myself. But I feel like you could use the chocolate cheer up."

"I don't *deserve* this cupcake!" I said, pushing the gooey-looking baked goodness away from me. "I put my two best friends in danger! It was a stupid, dumb, terrible idea."

Sandro made his lip quiver like he was going to cry. "Be nice to the cupcake, Peter," pleaded Sandro. "It's the last of its kind."

Chloe grabbed the scrumptious little morsel and waved it right in front of my face.

"You *do* deserve it. Eat the cupcake," said Chloe. "And relax. So you made a mistake. It's not the end of the world. You tried. You failed. You learned a lesson. On to the next adventure!"

"But I made you two come along," I said. "You could have been hurt."

"You didn't *make* us do anything," Chloe said. "We wanted to go."

"Yeah, you can't force me!" Sandro said. He flexed his tiny arm muscles. "No one can force me to do anything. Except my mom."

"Yeah?" I asked. I took a bite of the cupcake. It *was* delicious.

"Yeah, we're good, bro," Sandro said. "But if you're grounded, you should probably loan me some of your video games. You can borrow some comics from me in exchange." He added, "But if you want to feel down, that's okay too. I get down sometimes myself. Hanging out with you guys always makes me feel better."

I had expected Sandro and Chloe to be mad at me for getting them involved in such a big mess—but they weren't. They were comforting me, like they always did.

"Are you sure you two still want to be my friends?"

"Duh," Sandro said. "I don't share cupcakes with just anyone."

"Of course, Peter," Chloe said. "It's not like *we* got grounded."

"You two are my best friends," I confessed. "Sometimes I worry that my crummy powers will mess that up."

"That's not how friendship works, Peter," Chloe said. "We'd be your friends whether you have dumb powers, superpowers, or a big, rainbow unicorn horn."

"You should see if you can grow a rainbow unicorn horn. I bet they grant wishes!" said Sandro, his eyes growing wide thinking about it.

Chloe pointed to the little bit of chocolate deliciousness that was sitting in front of me. "Finish that," she said. "And let's come up with a plan to get your brother and sister to stop bothering you—but a plan *without* supervillains."

I ate the rest of the cupcake. I already felt better, thanks to my friends.

CHAPTER TEN
Off to the Moon

Having parents who are superheroes means that evenings can get a little hectic. Especially in the Powers household.

"The emergency numbers are on the fridge! You can have leftovers for dinner! WAIT! Where's your baby brother?!" Mom asked in a tizzy.

Some kids have parents who go on business trips. My parents are no different—if by "business trip" you mean "flying to the moon to stop a giant alien monster."

Yup. An alien was trying to eat the moon (again). My dad was already on his way, but Mom stayed behind to make sure her kids were okay. She needed to leave like five minutes ago!

"Ben is right over there," I said, pointing to my baby brother, who was cheerfully munching on his fingers. He wasn't invisible...at the moment.

"Where's Grandpa?! Where're Gavin and Felicia?! *UGH*. There's no time! I have to go! Peter, watch your brother! Make sure he eats! And goes to bed on time! You're in charge," Mom commanded.

"In charge?" I gulped. That sounded like a lot of responsibility.

"Don't worry, Mom. I can do this," I said, hoping to make her feel better. She had plenty to worry about—what with a monster alien eating the moon. (You could actually see a little red dot up in the sky if you looked hard enough.)

Not to mention, this might be my chance to turn things around. If I handled this evening well, maybe I could prove to my parents that I could handle any situation. Or at least deserved to be ungrounded early.

"Be careful, be safe, and keep an eye on everything!" my mom shouted as she flew out the back door. "Your dad and I trust you!"

It felt good to hear her say those words. Though I wondered if she actually meant them.

SWASH!! My mom shot into the sky faster than a rocket ship. She left a trail of smoke behind her.

I stared up at the moon and squinted. I bet she was already there. My parents really are amazing. I don't know how they juggle having a big family *and* saving the world every other week.

"Where are your parents?" Grandpa

asked. He was just waking up from a nap. He loved to sleep.

"The moon," I said. "Alien monster trying to eat it."

"Again?" Grandpa said. "Oh well. If your parents are gone, you know what that means?"

"Lots of chores and an early bedtime," I said, trying to be responsible.

"Nope. Time to party! HA-HA-HA!" Grandpa said. Then he rolled his wheelchair into the living room and flipped on the television. "Time to watch my shows! They have bad words."

Gavin and Felicia strolled into the house an hour later.

"Your mom left Peter in charge, so you better listen to him," Grandpa grunted.

"What?!" Felicia and Gavin yelped.

"Yeah, I'm in charge," I said. "So, that means we're all going to behave and not cause any trouble and take care of Ben and—"

"Where *is* Ben?" Felicia asked.

Uh-oh. I looked around the room. I didn't see him anywhere. He was just here a minute ago. *No need to panic*, I thought. Not *yet*, at least.

"Good job, Peter Pointless," Gavin said. "You lost our brother."

"Ben!" I shouted. I ran around the house listening for him. The worst part was that Ben thought this was a funny game. But hide-and-seek with an invisible baby is *not* fun for anybody. "Ben!!"

I made sure all the doors were closed and locked. Then I checked the stairs. Oh no. This was bad. "Grandpa, have you seen Ben?" I said in a panic. But Grandpa was already fast asleep in his wheelchair. He's the only person I know who can be wide awake one minute and sound asleep the next.

"Can you two help me?!" I asked.

"No, you're in charge. You find him," Gavin said. My brother and sister took seats on the couch and changed the channel.

"Turn up the TV," said Felicia, snatching the remote control from Gavin.

"*We interrupt this program to bring you an important news break,*" the TV said. "*Captain Tornado has been spotted at the famous Capital Bank in downtown Boulder City. The authorities advise everyone to stay clear of the area.*"

"*That's* the bad guy Peter tried to fight?" Gavin asked. "I could take him."

"He looks *puny* to me," Felicia said. She flexed. "I bet I could break him in half."

"Fighting a supervillain is harder than it sounds," I said. "Now can you please help me find Ben?"

"I don't think fighting a supervillain would be hard at all," Felicia said. "I mean, I'm super strong."

"And I can make ten of myself!" Gavin said.

I was so frustrated! Not just because Ben was missing, but because my brother and sister kept picking on me. Before I knew it, I was shouting at them. "You think you can beat Captain Tornado?

There's your chance!" I pointed to the TV.
"I'd love to see you try!"

"Oh yeah?" Gavin said.

"Yeah!" I replied. But then I took a deep
breath, like Mom always did. "No, don't
do it. It's dangerous. And you could get
really hurt."

Gavin and Felicia looked at each other
devilishly and ran toward the front door.
I beat them there and stood in the way.
But Felicia lifted me up straight over
her head.

"No no no!" I said. "You can't do this!
Captain Tornado is dangerous!"

"Don't worry about us," Felicia said
and smiled.

"Yeah. Worry about Ben," Gavin added. Then they ran off down the street.

They had to be playing. They couldn't really be going to fight Captain Tornado, not after all the trouble I'd gotten in. It was just a practical joke, I thought. Right?

Oh no. What did I just do? Were my siblings about to go take on Captain Tornado by themselves?! I looked down the street, but it was too late. They were gone.

My parents were fighting an alien. Ben was invisible and missing. And I had talked my siblings into fighting a super-villain. This was *bad*. If everyone survived tonight, I would be grounded for life.

CHAPTER ELEVEN
Taken Hostage

Okay, one problem at a time, I told myself. First, I needed to find my baby brother. Then I could worry about Gavin and Felicia.

"Ben! Where are you?!" I shouted.

"Ben go bye-bye!" a voice called out from the backyard.

As soon as I got there, I saw my baby brother turn invisible. But I was closing in on his location. He couldn't hide forever.

"Ben, no go bye-bye. Show yourself, please!"

I heard him giggle. I was worried about stepping on him, so I had to use my detective skills on this one. How do you find an invisible baby? First, check the place he loves the most! In Ben's case, that would be a pile of dirt in the backyard. As I tiptoed very carefully, I noticed some mud seemingly floating in midair. That was Ben, all right. He threw the mud, and it hit me in the face. He laughed.

"No more Ben go bye-bye!" I pleaded.

"Ben here," he said, turning visible. I scooped him up quickly. "Ben go bye-bye!" he said, turning invisible again. But at least I was holding him.

Ben poked me with his muddy fingers as I cleaned him off in the kitchen sink. He giggled until he farted too. Not surprising—he *is* a baby.

Now that I'd solved one problem, I could turn my attention to the big issue.

My sister and brother had been gone for almost an hour. My mind was racing. What was I supposed to do? Go after them?

I couldn't leave Ben alone, and Grandpa was still fast asleep.

Felicia and Gavin knew better than to try to stop Captain Tornado by themselves. Didn't they?

They may be crazy, but they're not *that* crazy. I figured that they were hiding somewhere, waiting until Mom and Dad got home. Then they'd pop out and get me in trouble. Yes, that's what they were doing. Sometimes I wish I were an only child. So the best thing I could do was take care of Ben and wait. That was the responsible thing to do. So why was I so nervous?

"GOOD MORNING!" Grandpa shouted,

perking up from his deep sleep. "Did I miss my stories? Did Lance finally kiss Angelica? I've been waiting for that moment ever since I started watching *Love Nest!*" Have I mentioned my grandpa watches the freakiest TV shows?

"I turned the TV off, Grandpa. There's been a…" I struggled to find the right words. How do I tell him that I lost my baby brother for an hour, and my other siblings ran off to fight a crazy super-villain? I sheepishly said, "Some stuff happened while you were sleeping."

"Nothing too exciting, I hope," Grandpa said, grabbing the remote control. "Let's see what's on the boob tube!" I don't know why he calls the television the boob tube, but it always makes me laugh. What came next, however, did *not* make me laugh.

The TV announced, *"We have an update on the Captain Tornado situation that's been developing at the Capital Bank in downtown Boulder City. After the building was evacuated, police set up a perimeter to try to negotiate with Captain Tornado. But it seems two children somehow entered the scene to confront the dastardly supervillain directly. They seem to be unharmed at this time, but they have been taken hostage. More on this situation as it develops."*

That's when the camera zoomed in on the bank. Through the window, you could see Gavin and Felicia, caught in a tornado.

Grandpa squinted at the TV. "Those little rascals on the TV look like your brother and sister," he said suspiciously. "How about you tell me what's going on, Peter? And start at the beginning."

I told Grandpa everything. He wasn't as mad as I thought he was going to be. As a matter of fact, the look in his eye made me think he was a little bit *excited*.

"Well, I guess it's time for ol' Grandpa Dale to clean things up, just like the old days. Pull your pants up, Peter. We're going for a ride. *It's old-school hero time!*"

CHAPTER TWELVE
Night Flight

"Wheel me outside, Peter," Grandpa said, motioning to the door. "Hurry! We don't have all night!" Grandpa was planning something, but I couldn't figure out what it was. Holding on to Ben, I pushed Grandpa's wheelchair outside.

"I don't know if this is a good time for a spin around the block, Grandpa," I said. "Maybe we should wait for Mom and Dad—"

"C'mon, boy! This is a life-or-death

situation!" he commanded. Life or death? I wish he hadn't said that. *But okay*, I thought, *Grandpa knows best*. I pushed him out to the front lawn.

"Now help me stand up." Grandpa took a moment to get his balance. His legs were pretty shaky, since he doesn't walk a lot these days. He took a deep breath and held it until his face turned bright red. I was worried his head might pop off!

Instead, something amazing happened: A pair of *giant wings* burst out of Grandpa's back. They must have been ten feet long. EACH! I couldn't believe it. I knew Grandpa used to have superpowers,

but this was more awesome than I could
ever have imagined.

"Grandpa, you've got wings!" I said,
amazed.

"WHAT?! WHERE?! GET 'EM OFF!!" he
shouted, shaking his body all around like
he was doing the hokey pokey. "HA-HA!
I'm only playing with you. Of course
I've got wings! I used to be a superhero

back in the day. We're going to save your sister and brother, Peter. Secure Ben and hold tight. Things can get pretty windy up there."

I put on the baby harness and strapped Ben into it as tightly as I could. Visible or not, he wasn't getting loose again—that much I knew for sure.

Then I hopped on Grandpa's back and held on. He flapped his wings and took off like a hawk. I didn't know if I was scared or amazed—actually, I think I was a little of both.

"You can see the whole town from up here," I said.

"When I was your age, I rarely had

my feet on the ground. I always loved to soar above the clouds. Nowadays, my wings wear me out, so I don't use them much," he said, reminiscing. "Makes me miss your grandma, but she's with us in spirit. She might even be up here with us right now."

Grandpa didn't talk about Grandma much, but every time he did, it made him smile bigger than ever.

"Geeeeeeee!" Ben giggled, the wind blowing his baby slobber all over my face. (Being a big brother means getting lots of gross things on your face.)

"We're almost there, Peter. Prepare yourself for landing!" Grandpa wheezed.

He was out of breath. The ride was over before it had barely begun. That was *quick*.

We landed safely behind the Capital Bank. But as soon as our feet were on the ground, Grandpa lay down. "Whew! That took it out of me," he said. "I'm not used to this much action."

"Are you going to be okay?" I asked, worried.

"Kid, I used to battle robots as big as buildings. A little flight across town ain't gonna do me in. Now, give me your brother. I'll watch Ben while you become the hero you're meant to be."

"Grandpa, I'm not sure if you heard,

but my superpowers aren't exactly super."

"Listen up. It isn't what you have, it's what's in your heart. Now, you go in there and don't back down. You are a *hero*, Gavin. Use your clone power and show that bad guy you're the boss!"

"Grandpa, it's *me*, Peter," I reminded him.

"*Who?*" Grandpa asked. His memory can be a little spotty sometimes.

"I'M *PETER POWERS!* I HAVE

THE POWER TO CREATE *ICE CUBES*!"
I said loudly enough for the whole town
to hear. Grandpa started giggling that
mischievous little giggle of his. Then he
gave me a serious look.

"I know who you are, Peter. I just
wanted you to hear yourself say it out
loud, and with pride. Now get in there
and be a superhero!"

I rolled up my sleeves, put on my
homemade mask, pulled my hood over my
head, and stormed toward the bank.

There was no turning back now.

CHAPTER THIRTEEN
The Big Battle

I pushed open the back door of the bank like a boss! It gave me kind of a rush. I guess Grandpa's pep talk worked. But where was Captain Tornado? I scanned the lobby and spotted Gavin and Felicia—they were spinning in circles, each trapped in a mini-tornado!

Meanwhile, Captain Tornado was in the vault, counting the money with the help of more little tornadoes.

Quietly, I snuck over to my siblings in

the shadows, careful not to alert Captain Tornado to my presence.

"Are you okay?" I whispered.

"Yeah, just too dizzy to multiply," Gavin said. He looked green from vertigo.

"And I can't use my super strength when I'm stuck in a storm," Felicia muttered. "That's the only reason I haven't kicked his butt yet, in case you're wondering."

"I'm just glad you're safe," I whispered. "I'm sorry that I dared you to do this. It was dumb of me."

"Well, we were the ones who came," Gavin said. "It's not all your fault."

"It's ours too," Felicia agreed.

"That's actually quite touching," said Captain Tornado, emerging from the vault. "My family is *never* that nice to one another."

"We meet again, Captain Tornado!" I said, trying to make my voice sound as tough as I could. "Release these innocents right now, or you're going to have a *big* problem!"

I was shaking in my shoes, but only a little. Captain Tornado sighed. "Kid, come on. We've been over this. You make ice cubes. I can conjure tornadoes. You're no match for me. Please go home before you get hurt."

The supervillain went right back into the vault. He was using his wind powers to put money in large bags. A giant tower of money flowed into his bag with ease. I had to admit, I was jealous of Captain Tornado's awesome powers.

"Captain Tornado, time to face me!" I said as threateningly as possible. But my voice cracked. (It happens. I'm a growing boy.)

"Okay, fine," he said with a sigh. "If you really insist on fighting, I guess I'll give you one round. Come on. Give me your best shot."

He didn't think I was a threat. I was genuinely insulted. I'd show him!

I concentrated as hard as I could.

This was my big moment. I know I'd thought that before, but I swear this time it was real. I could feel my body charging itself with ice power.

The feeling kept growing and growing. I felt like I was about to explode. When I couldn't wait any longer, I pointed my hands at Captain Tornado and let loose!

A dozen small ice cubes shot out across the floor in front of him. Most of them didn't even hit him. They landed at his toes.

"Oh man, kid," Captain Tornado said. "Ice making? That's rough. And I thought my powers were lame."

"You do?"

"Well, not now, but when I was younger," Tornado said, walking over to me. "I went to school at Villain Academy, and kids were *mean*! They were always saying how crummy and dumb my powers were."

"That's what my brother and sister say about me all the time!" I said.

"But I worked hard, and eventually I made my wind power into tornado power. And now I've shown them. Most of those jerks are locked up in jail, or stuck with boring desk jobs. Me? All I do is rob banks every few years and then spend the rest of my time on vacation. My point is, keep at it. You'll get there."

He added, "Try to keep in mind, you don't need great superpowers to be great. My brother doesn't have any powers, and he's a successful banker! It's not about *what* you have, it's about *what you do* with what you have."

Was I really getting another pep talk from this supervillain?

"Thanks," I said. "You seem like a good guy—so I'll tell you what. If you leave now, out the back door, I won't call the cops for five minutes."

"Come on, kid," Tornado said. "Game over. You can't beat me."

"But I have to try," I said, hoping I seemed commanding enough. "That money isn't yours to take. Other people worked for it, and they keep it here so it's safe. And this town is under my protection."

Captain Tornado sighed. "I guess I'm going to have to fight you, then." But as he took a step toward me, he slipped on some of my ice. He lost his balance and flew wildly into the air, doing three—no, four!—flips. He landed flat on his back with a giant *CRACK!*

"MY BACK!" he shouted. All the tornadoes suddenly vanished. "I can't move! I twisted my back. *Ouch ouch ouch...*"

Did this mean I had won?

"Peter, you did it! You stopped Captain Tornado!" shouted Felicia.

"I don't believe my eyes. You actually did it," said Gavin, his jaw dropping in disbelief.

I stopped Captain Tornado. *I STOPPED CAPTAIN TORNADO!* I felt like nothing could ruin this moment.

That is, until Mom and Dad showed up.

CHAPTER FOURTEEN
A Bad Break

Mom and Dad slowly stepped into the bank, surveying the scene. I was nervous and excited. Would they be proud of me for defeating a supervillain, or would they be mad at me for getting involved in a dangerous situation?

Mom had the same look on her face that she gets when she opens the door to my room and sees how messy it is. There were dollar bills everywhere! Captain Tornado was lying on the floor of the bank, whispering *"ouch ouch ouch"* over and over again. Dad walked over to him and made sure he was down for the count.

And he totally *was*.

"So how was the moon?" I asked. I thought it would be a nice icebreaker.

"The moon was fine, thank you," Mom said. "Care to explain what's going on here?"

"Peter *kind of* stopped the bad guy," Felicia said reluctantly. I could tell she didn't want to admit that. I could also tell that she was hoping our parents wouldn't find out that she and Gavin tried to fight a supervillain.

"He didn't do what *I* would have done, but, yeah, Peter took out Captain Tornado,

I guess," Gavin said, shrugging. He was so jealous, I could tell. Then Grandpa hobbled into the bank with baby Ben in tow and sang my praises loud and proud.

"You did it, boy! You saved the day!" Grandpa shouted, handing Ben to Mom and throwing his hands up in the air. "Someone is going to have to carry me home. My wings are so sore!"

"Thanks for keeping an eye on the kids, Dale," Dad said, rolling his eyes.

"You're welcome," Grandpa said.

"I was being sarcastic," Dad growled.

"What do you want from me? I'm an old man. Peter did fine. Especially since *those* little troublemakers are the ones who started this whole mess," Grandpa said, pointing at Felicia and Gavin. There was no way they could escape now.

"Uh, it was Gavin's idea," whined Felicia.

"Uh, it was Felicia's idea," whined Gavin.

"You're both grounded," Mom said, frustrated. "For *two* months."

"We're going to have a talk about all this once we get home," Mom said. She stared at me for a moment. I thought she might yell. I *really* hoped she wouldn't yell. "Thank you for looking out for your brothers and sister, Peter. I can't believe it. My little boy is growing up!" What a *mom* thing to say. She hugged me.

"*Excuse me?*" whimpered Captain Tornado. "Would you mind taking me to a doctor? I think I hurt my back." Dad walked over and knelt down beside Captain Tornado like he was going to tell him a secret.

"Why don't we take you to the *police station* instead?" Dad suggested.

"I thought you might say that. Just be careful of *MY BACK*," grumbled Captain Tornado, wincing in pain.

Dad gently scooped up Captain Tornado, put him over his shoulder, and took him outside. The cops were waiting with an ambulance nearby.

By the time we got home, Grandpa and Ben were fast asleep. Gavin and Felicia were bickering. And Mom and Dad couldn't stop smiling at me. What a crazy day.

CHAPTER FIFTEEN
A New Beginning

The following morning, I arrived at the breakfast table feeling pretty darn good. Nothing was going to mess up my day. *NOT A SINGLE THING.*

"Hey, *squirt!*" said Gavin, blowing a raspberry as I walked by. Normally, I would have rolled my eyes, but today I was taking it all in stride.

"I'm the squirt that saved *your* behind!" I said with a grin.

"You stopped Captain Tornado *by*

accident," Felicia said. "Don't act like you planned anything. You're not some big superhero now, Peter." She was partially right, but that didn't matter, not today at least. Today I was a hero, and that was good enough for me.

"If it wasn't for Peter, you'd both still be stuck in a tornado at the bank," Mom said, eyeing Felicia and Gavin. "Perhaps you should show him a little respect." She finished strapping baby Ben into his high chair and was ready to serve breakfast when the day took a slight detour.

"Honey, I just got a call from Commissioner Jenkins," Dad said, running down the stairs, out of breath. "There's a fire down by the pier. We've got to get there fast!" Normally, my parents did their superhero thing at night, but emergencies happen at all hours.

"You'll have to go without me. I've got to feed the baby, then get the kids to school on time," Mom said. She was a little frustrated, and it gave me an idea.

"I'll help you, Dad!" I said enthusiastically. The room fell silent. They clearly didn't share my excitement. Gavin looked at me like I'd farted. Felicia looked at Gavin like I had spiders crawling out of my eye sockets. Mom looked at Dad like her head was about to explode. But Dad smiled.

"That's a lot of responsibility," Dad said firmly.

"I know. But I've thought about this a lot, and I want to learn from the best," I said. "I'll never go out and try to be a hero on my own. Not until I'm older. And not until I've had some training."

Mom eyed Dad. Gavin and Felicia rolled their eyes and fidgeted in their seats like they had poison ivy.

"It's nice to finally have a kid who's interested in what his parents do," Dad smiled. "Go grab a clean cape and a fresh mask. But you're only watching. And this is *just for today*. You still have to go to school after I put out the fire."

I couldn't believe it. He had said YES.
I could barely contain myself. I was so
excited, I thought I was going to burst
open like a piñata. Candy and prizes
would fly everywhere!

"I think training is a good idea," Dad
said, patting me on the back. "Stay on the
sidelines

and watch
what I do.
This could
get very
dangerous."

"Listen to
your father,

honey," Mom said, kissing me on my forehead. "Being a superhero isn't easy, but it's time you started learning." My mom is *awesome*. Guess who wasn't so supportive?

"It's not fair!" protested Felicia.

"Good luck, *SQUIRT*! You'll need it," threatened Gavin.

Not even my salty siblings could ruin this moment. I was finally ready to start my new life as a superhero sidekick. Dad gave me a nod, and we were on our way.

"See you later, Gavin!" I said, strolling out the door. "Bye, Felicia!"

Look out, world, here comes Peter Powers, superhero in training!

"Peter, you forgot your cape and mask!" Mom called out.

One step at a time, I thought. *One day I'll get there.*